Jamaica in my Tummy

By Jean Hawthorn-DaCosta / Illustrated by Justin Stier

Published by Mindstir Media LLC

45 Lafayette Rd. Suite 181 | North Hampton, NH 03862 | USA

1.800.767.0531 | www.mindstirmedia.com

Printed in the United States of America

ISBN-13: 978-0-9990698-1-3

Library of Congress Control Number: 2017908403

"Wake up child, we have a long journey to go on today", my grandmother said. She placed a cup of hot chocolate beside me. The hot chocolate smelled so good! When I took a sip, it was rich and sweet and so yummy in my tummy.

"Where are we going today, Grandma?"

Grandma smiled and replied, "Oh, just through the plains, up the hills, around a couple bends and corners through Jamaica until we reach to good old Portland.

"Eat your breakfast first, then we shall head out".

Grandma put a plate of hot ackee and saltfish, fried ripe plantains and a golden round Johnny dumpling in front of me. It was so yummy in my tummy.

I loved to travel with Grandma. She always brought the yummiest snacks to eat and there was plenty to see.

"Off we go", said Grandma, and off we went.

"Care for a little something to munch on honey? Grandma asked.

"Oh yes Grandma".

Grandma took out a most special treat out of her basket. It was a white square with a pink dot on the middle. "Oh Grandma! How did you know I love grater cake?" I asked as I unwrapped it from the plastic bag. Grater cake is a favourite treat of mine, it is so sweet and so yummy in my tummy.

"Here we are in St. Elizabeth", Grandma said. Grandma's best friend lived here on a farm. Miss June grew all kinds of crops, like escallion, thyme, tomatoes and my favourite, mangoes. Whenever we came for a visit, Miss June would give me the sweetest mango for myself. It was a special East Indian Mango she grew.

"Yummy", I told her before I took another bite of the juicy fruit.

It was soon time to leave Miss June, but I loved Manchester too, so I was not sad.

Soon the air was fresher; we were in cool, cool Manchester. Best of all, it was lunch time. Off to Claudette's Curry Shop we went. Grandma ordered our lunch. The waiter brought a tray with two plates of steaming curry goat and hot white rice and a tall glass of cold lemonade. My mouth watered. Lunch was just yummy in my tummy.

Grandma went to pay the bill. Miss Claudette came out to say hello and to collect some goods from Grandma.

"Hello little lady. How are you today? Did you enjoy your lunch?" Miss Claudette asked.

"Of course, Miss Claudette", I replied with a big smile.

"Well then, I have a special treat for you". Miss Claudette gave me a napkin with a small piece of potato pudding.

"Thank you, Miss Claudette", I said, as I gave her a big hug.

On the way to the van I took a little taste of the potato pudding. It was yummy in my tummy delicious.

Off we went again on our journey.

"Clarendon, here we come", Grandma shouted and started the van.

Soon we were driving down a steep hill and there were mountains and hills everywhere.

"Wake up child", Grandma gently shook me. "We have reached to Uncle Ted's farm in Clarendon".

While Grandma and Uncle Ted loaded the van with ripe watermelons, I played with my cousins, Philip and Izzy. We played a game of hide and seek and some jump rope. Philip was the best seeker. No matter where Izzy and I hid, he found us. What fun it was!

"Anyone for a snack"? Uncle Ted yelled.

"Yes", we all shouted.

Uncle Ted had bought beef patties for us in brown paper bags. Izzy was too little to eat a whole patty by herself so I shared mine with her. The beef was hot and the crust was crispy and it was quite yummy in my tummy.

Soon the sky started to get dark and Grandma said it was time to go.

We began the last leg of our journey to the last stop, Portland.

We passed lots of fruit trees along the way and saw people gathered by stalls with huge pots eating boiled corn.

"Jamaica sure has a lot of delicious food, eh Grandma"?

"Yes my child, lots and lots of delicious food to fill our tummies".

Finally we reached to Portland. It was dinner time at Auntie Susie. She had cooked jerked pork and festival.

"Hungry?" She asked.

I looked at the jerked pork and festival and then down at my tummy. I was still full. I had drunk and eaten my way from Westmoreland to Portland. I had drunk and eaten hot chocolate, ackee and saltfish, fried ripe plantain, Johnny dumpling, grater cake, pineapple watermelon, curry goat and rice, lemonade, potato pudding and beef patty.

I had Jamaica in my tummy!

"Maybe tomorrow, Auntie Susie", I said, rubbing my very full tummy. Today I perhaps had a little too much Jamaica in my tummy. Grandma and Auntie Susie laughed.

Making Johnny Dumplings

Johnny Dumplings are easy and quick to make. Some persons call them "Fried Dumpling". When fresh from the pan, they go well with a little butter or my children's favorite, strawberry jam. Some persons cut it in half after it is cooked and put calalloo, ackee or just about anything that can fit inside and it is eaten like a tiny little sandwich. A Jamaican favorite is also to dip the dumpling in porridge and eat heartily.

Instructions to Make Johnny Dumplings

Ingredients

2 cups All Purpose Flour

½ teaspoon salt (or a pinch as my granny would say)

3 teaspoons Baking Powder

3 tablespoons Butter (room temperature)

¾ cups Water

½ cup Cooking Oil (Vegetable Oil works well for us)

Instructions

1. Grab an adult.

2. Combine flour, salt and baking powder in a bowl.

3. Add and mix in butter into the dry ingredients with your hands until crumbly.

4. Add water, a little at a time until mixture becomes a dough. If it already forms a nice dough perhaps you may not need all the water.

5. Leave dough aside for about 15 minutes or so.

6. Shape dough into small balls or have fun with it and make different shapes. As children we made the letters of our names or hearts.

7. Pour oil into the frying pan so that it reaches about half the sides of the dumplings. The flame should be medium. Wait until oil is hot and carefully place dumplings inside the pan.

8. Fry each side of the dumplings until golden brown. When fully cooked they will be golden brown on the outside and have a hollow sound.

9. Rest dumplings on a plate for a little to cool a bit before eating.

CPSIA information can be obtained
at www.ICGtesting.com
Printed in the USA
LVHW01n0047250818
588091LV00002B/5/P